oloo

Llama ᴵᴺ ᴛʜᴇ Library

BY JOHANNA HURWITZ

The Adventures of Ali Baba Bernstein
Aldo Applesauce
Aldo Ice Cream
Aldo Peanut Butter
Ali Baba Bernstein, Lost and Found
Baseball Fever
Birthday Surprises: Ten Great Stories to Unwrap
Busybody Nora
Class Clown
Class President
The Cold & Hot Winter
DeDe Takes Charge!
The Down & Up Fall
"E" Is for Elisa
Elisa in the Middle
Even Stephen
Ever-Clever Elisa
Faraway Summer
The Hot & Cold Summer
Hurray for Ali Baba Bernstein
Hurricane Elaine
The Law of Gravity
A Llama in the Family

Llama In The Library

JOHANNA HURWITZ

illustrated by
MARK GRAHAM

MORROW JUNIOR BOOKS

NEW YORK

Published by Morrow Junior Books
a division of William Morrow and Company, Inc.
1350 Avenue of the Americas, New York, NY 10019
www.williammorrow.com

Printed in the United States of America.

10   9   8   7   6   5   4   3   2   1

Library of Congress Cataloging-in-Publication Data
Hurwitz, Johanna.
Llama in the library/Johanna Hurwitz; illustrated by Mark Graham.
p. cm.
Summary: Fifth-grader Adam Fine thinks that his two llamas will be
a hit at the grand reopening of the town's library.
ISBN 0-688-16138-3
[1. Llamas—Fiction.   2. Ghosts—Fiction.   3. Babies—Fiction.]
I. Graham, Mark, ill.   II. Title.
PZ7.H9575Ln 1999   [Fic]—dc21   98-34374   CIP AC

For the new Mrs. Hurwitz:
Kimberly Elizabeth Bogdan Hurwitz
With love from the old one

CONTENTS

Llama In The Library

1
An "Event of Nature"

When I walked into school on the first Friday of September, a voice called out to me. "Hey, Adam, do you know what day this is?" Of course I knew.

In my school in Wilmington, Vermont, the same thing always happens on the first Friday of September. It's a day that every fifth grader has joked about and waited for, and it's not because it will be followed by the weekend. Every year on the first Friday of September the fifth-grade boys and girls are separated from each other, and everyone gets to see a video about sex.

"Today's not Friday, it's Sexday," Ryan announced to all of us when he walked into our classroom that morning.

Of course, living out in the country as we do, almost all of us have seen animals reproducing around us. Gary's family has a dairy farm, and he has helped when the calves are born in the spring. Kim's grandparents raise goats over in Putney. Ryan's parents breed dogs. And almost everyone has a cat that gave birth to kittens or a few chickens hatching eggs. So we know a lot about the subject of reproduction already.

It seems silly not to let everyone sit together in a classroom to discuss reproduction. But I guess it's one thing to understand about chickens and kittens and another thing to look at a video with cartoons of a naked human male and female.

Later in the morning, when the boys were sitting on the floor of the darkened gym watching the video, there was a lot of whispering and giggling. I heard at least two kids saying "Gross!" under their breath when the cartoon male's sperm traveled up the vagina of the cartoon woman.

"Bingo!" someone called out when one of the sperm succeeded in uniting with the waiting egg cell.

Mr. Hanford, our phys ed teacher, had already turned the lights on once to be sure everyone was paying attention and not getting silly about what he called "these important events of nature."

So this time he ignored the outburst and let the video continue. We watched as the cells multiplied and became a human embryo. We learned that when the sperm cell and the egg cell join together, the result is smaller than a period at the end of a sentence. I wanted to stop the tape right then and think about it a bit. Imagine being smaller than a dot!

The video went on. At the age of forty days the embryo weighs less than a book of paper matches. After eight weeks the unborn baby is called a fetus.

"That's when the feet develop," a voice called out, and once again there was a lot of giggling.

It takes a long time for a human baby to grow—much longer than for a chick or a kitten or a lot of other kinds of animals. Of course, the video speeded up the events, and within ten minutes a baby was born.

"I know all about this stuff already," Ryan boasted in the dark.

"I'm glad we're not girls," my best friend, Justin, whispered in my ear. "Who'd want to go through all that?"

"Well, luckily our mothers were willing, or we wouldn't be sitting here right now," I pointed out

to him. But he was right. I wouldn't want to be a girl either.

Despite all the talking during the video, when it was over and we had the chance to ask questions, all of us felt much too self-conscious to say anything. It was even worse when we were back in the classroom with the girls. They'd been watching another print of that same video in the lunchroom. No one wanted to look anyone else in the eye, and there were lots of red faces and muffled giggles. I'm sure every guy in fifth grade was thinking the same thing: Which of them would I ever want to do *it* with? When Mrs. Wurst told us to take out our math books, for once we were *glad* it was math time.

Most of us fifth graders have known one another since kindergarten. Over the years we've learned which kids we like and which we'd just as soon never see again. It's only when someone new moves to town that there are a few surprises. This year there's a new girl in our class—Alana Brown. Her last name may be Brown, but she's got long blond hair, which she always wears in a single thick braid down her back. I haven't really talked to her at all, but sometimes I catch myself watching her. Like on the first day of school, the principal had stopped in our classroom to greet all of us.

"Last year you had bales of work," he'd said,

"but soon you'll discover that fifth grade is the worst."

Right away Alana and I laughed at this pun on our teacher's name. It took the other kids a couple of seconds to catch on. Afterward I realized that Alana probably didn't even understand all of the principal's joke. Our fourth-grade teacher was Mrs. *Bayles.*

Anyhow, I don't know if it's because she's new or because there's something special about her, but I think I like Alana a little. Just a little. I can't imagine making a baby with her, or with anyone, ever. But I would like to squeeze that long golden braid of hers, just once.

Now here's the amazing thing that happened. That very same evening I was sitting in the living room watching a baseball game on TV. Our cat, Molly Stark, was on my lap, and my parents were sitting on the sofa watching the game too. My little sister, April, was upstairs, asleep in bed. It was the seventh-inning stretch, and the Red Sox were so far behind that there didn't seem to be a chance in the world of their winning. I put Molly Stark down on the floor and stood up.

"Adam," my dad said, "we hear you saw a film in school about babies. As a matter of fact, your mother and I have some good news on that subject ourselves."

6

"Yeah?" I asked. Since I was a Red Sox fan, I really needed some good news at that moment.

"You're going to be a big brother again," Mom said.

"Again?" I asked. I was only six years old when April was born. Actually, April's a cute kid, and most of the time I don't mind her at all. But now the noise and mess and confusion of a new baby would start all over again at our house.

Then I thought, My parents had done that stuff I'd seen on the video. I tried to imagine my dad's sperm inside my mother. All right, I thought. So they had to do it to make me. And sure, once they had a boy they wanted a girl. But why do *it* again? What did they think they'd get this time?

"We aren't going to tell April about it for a bit," my mother said. "The baby isn't due until early April, and that will be much too long for her to have to think about it. Even a week seems to take forever when you're four years old. So we'll keep this a secret from her for now, but we wanted to share the news with you right away."

"It won't be a secret for long." My father grinned, and he leaned over and patted my mother's stomach. Mom smiled back at him. Soon she would have a big fat tummy that would be the embryo growing inside her. I turned my head to watch the commercial on the TV screen so they wouldn't notice me turning red.

As expected, the Red Sox lost the game. I went up to bed, and just before I fell asleep, I thought about what Justin had whispered in my ear while we were watching the video. Thank goodness I was born a boy.

2
The Other
White House

The next morning I thought about the new baby as I sat eating breakfast. I wondered how it might change things in our lives. Mostly things were pretty good for me. I had spent the entire summer vacation bonding with our pet llama. And the summer had concluded with my getting both a second llama for our family and the gift of a mountain bike for myself. I almost didn't get that bike, because money was a bit tight just now. A new baby would bring new expenses, I realized. Luckily my mom had started her llama trekking business, and it seemed to be growing more successful all the time.

I was just wondering how long it took for a baby llama to develop when Justin peeked through the screen door that leads into the kitchen. He called out hi and walked right inside. That's how at home we feel at each other's houses. But even though he was my best friend, I'd already decided that I wasn't going to tell him that my mother was pregnant. At least not for a while. After yesterday's video he'd tease me something fierce. I'd wait a few weeks until those cartoons had faded a little in our memory.

"Morning, Justin," my mother said. "I'll put another English muffin into the toaster for you."

"What's that gook you're putting on your muffin?" Justin asked, pointing to my breakfast.

I looked down at the jar I was holding with its pale yellow contents. "Dandelion jelly," I told him. "My mom made it last spring. Didn't you ever have any here before?"

"That's not what it looks like to me," Justin said as his muffin halves popped up from the toaster.

"It does look a little like honey," I admitted, biting into my muffin. "It even tastes like honey."

Justin leaned close to me. "It looks like a jar of piss," he whispered.

I gave him a jab with my elbow. Luckily my mother didn't seem to have heard him. She likes

Justin, but she sure wouldn't have liked him speaking that way in our kitchen.

"Don't you have any of your strawberry jam, Mrs. Fine? You make the best strawberry jam of anyone," he told my mom.

"I appreciate your flattery," my mother said. "But I don't feel up to going down to the basement to get the strawberry preserves. Try the dandelion jelly. I think you'll like it."

"Yeah. Close your eyes if you have to," I muttered to Justin, but he ate his muffin with butter instead.

April walked into the kitchen, still in her pajamas and still half-asleep.

"Oh, goody. Dandelion jelly," she said when she saw what I was eating. It made me laugh. Like I said, April's a cute kid.

"Don't forget the llamas," my mother called to me as Justin and I got up from the table.

"Mom, you know I'd never forget them," I protested.

My mom is proud of her business: She takes tourists on hikes. She packs a picnic lunch for everyone, and Ethan Allen and Ira Allen, our llamas, carry the food. The tourists go gaga over those two animals of ours. No wonder. Llamas are very lovable. They're gentle, handsome, clean, and fun.

"I've got a great plan for us for today," Justin announced as we walked out into the yard. "We're going looking for ghosts."

"Come off it," I responded, tipping over the huge bucket that held water for the llamas.

"Really," Justin insisted. I turned on the outside tap, and Justin hosed fresh water into the pail for Ethan and Ira. "Last night my father told me about a ghost up at the White House."

Before you decide that the president of the United States has a problem, let me tell you that the White House Justin was talking about is not the famous one in Washington, D.C. It just so happens that we have our own White House here in Wilmington. It's a big inn for tourists. I've never been inside, but my father took my mother there for dinner to celebrate their wedding anniversary last year. They said the food was great, but they never said anything about a ghost.

"How come we never heard about a ghost there before?" I asked Justin. "If there really was anything spooky going on so close to our homes, wouldn't we know about it?"

"My dad says they don't want to frighten the guests away. Think about it. Would you want to stay in a strange town and share a hotel room with a ghost?"

I laughed. Ethan Allen had begun drinking

some of the fresh water. He lifted his head and looked at me with his intelligent gaze. Then he lowered his head and continued drinking.

"Even our llama knows there's no such thing as a ghost," I said. "Next I suppose you'll tell me that your dog, Matty, is a really a werewolf. You've been reading too many of those horror books."

"Come on," said Justin. "Let's bike over to the White House. What can we lose?"

"Can we just walk in?" I asked him. Why would a fancy tourist inn let a pair of kids wander around inside looking for ghosts?

"You could take some of your mom's flyers. It would give us a perfect excuse for going there. Tell them that you just want to drop them off," Justin explained. "Only once we're there, we can ask to see the inside. We could say we'd always wanted to look around, since it's so famous."

Justin had a point. My mom had had an ad made for her llama trips. It's printed in the *Valley News*, our weekly newspaper, but she also had several hundred copies of it printed up on bright yellow paper, which we distributed around town.

"Okay," I said. I ran into the house and grabbed a handful of the flyers. "You've got to fill me in on everything your dad told you," I insisted to Justin.

So as we rode our bikes along toward the

White House, Justin told me all the details.

"The White House was built before the First World War by a man named Martin Brown who had piles of money. His wife, Clara, just loved the house. They lived there for almost fifty years, except of course it wasn't called the White House then. I'm not sure the house was even painted white in those days either. Mr. Brown died in 1962."

"That's the year my dad was born," I said. It seemed like a long time ago to me.

"Well, Clara Brown was pretty old herself by then, and everyone thought she'd sell the house. But she loved it so much that she insisted on living there alone," said Justin.

"And did she?" I asked.

"Yep. She stayed there for another ten years until she died too. She was ninety-five years old. Then the house got sold, and it became an inn. But my dad said it's claimed that the spirit of Clara Brown remains inside the house. Lots of times there are unexplained noises. Sometimes the doors slam shut when there isn't a breeze or anything to cause them to. Windows bang closed all by themselves. Weird things like that."

"Justin," I said, "that's crazy. They have two big collies at the White House, Eleanor and Rosie. Everybody knows about those dogs. Their picture is in all the ads. I bet one of the dogs bumped into a door and shut it."

"Yeah? Could a dog make a window shut itself too?" Justin asked.

"Maybe the window sash broke," I said. There had to be an explanation. I refused to believe that there was a ghost haunting the White House. Still, I was curious to see the inside of the place. I've only gone past it about a hundred thousand times.

3
"Fly Away Home"

After making our way up a couple of steep hills, we finally reached our White House. It may not be as famous as its namesake in Washington, but it's still a pretty neat house. More a mansion than a house, I guess. No ordinary family would live in a place with so many bedrooms and an almost equal number of baths. There were just a few cars parked in the driveway. I figured most of the guests were already off sight-seeing for the day. The dogs came up to inspect us, but they were accustomed to strangers, so they didn't bark; instead they wagged their tails happily when we gave them each a friendly pat.

"Let's leave our bikes here," said Justin, pointing to a place near the side of the house.

My bike is still so new that I'm a little nervous about just leaving it anywhere, even with the padlock on it. But you can't go about holding on to your bike all day long, so I got off and attached the lock. Then I removed the yellow flyers from the saddlebag on the back and followed Justin.

Inside the door we could smell bacon and coffee and other good breakfast smells. We could hear the tinkle of dishes too. Obviously a few of the guests were still finishing their morning meal. No one stopped us, so Justin and I just kept on walking.

"Quick," said Justin, pointing to a flight of stairs. "Let's go up."

But for a few seconds I just stood looking with amazement at the high ceilings and the fancy chandelier hanging down. The stairs were covered with such a thick pile that I couldn't even hear Justin's footsteps as he ran up them. I wondered who had gotten the contract to carpet this huge place. My dad owns Fine Carpet & Tile on Route 100. It would have been a great job for him.

At the top of the stairs we could see many doors. Most were closed. Justin walked over to an open door and walked inside, and I followed him.

I was nervous, not because of ghosts but because we were intruding.

Inside the room there was a huge unmade bed and luckily no sign of any occupant present. Another door inside the room led to its bathroom. The room still seemed damp from the shower a guest had recently taken, and there were wet towels on the floor. You'd think someone who had the money to stay at a place like this would know enough to hang up his towels. If it was the ghost, it sure had bad habits, I thought. My mom would have a fit if I left our bathroom in such a mess.

"Look," I said, picking up a tiny red ladybug with black spots off the sink. "I wonder how she got here."

"And if she had a reservation?" Justin added.

"Ladybug, ladybug, fly away home," I chanted, remembering a nursery rhyme in one of April's books at home.

"Are you looking for someone?" a voice asked.

I don't know who jumped higher, Justin or I. It wasn't a ghost speaking; it was a woman. She looked familiar. Maybe I've seen her in the supermarket or in the post office.

"Uh, uh, not exactly," said Justin. He'd lost all the confidence he'd had when we'd entered the place.

"Well, make yourselves useful. We've got a big

problem here," the woman said. "This place is overrun with—"

"Ghosts?" asked Justin hopefully.

"I wish it were ghosts," the woman said. "This is much worse. People like ghosts. They think that's interesting. But this just gets them upset. Especially the older women." She went to the window and pointed to the sill. "They're all over," the woman said.

"Ladybugs!" I called out when I saw the little red insects that must have been the sisters or aunts of the little bug still resting on my finger.

"It's like a huge convention of them," the woman complained. "They're everywhere. They're looking for someplace warm to hibernate."

Sure enough, now that she'd called our attention to them, I began noticing some on the curtains and on the bedside table and on the wall. Those little critters must reproduce like wild, I thought. Not one at a time like my mom.

"Whatever you do, don't kill them," the woman said as Justin started picking a few of them up off the windowsill and putting them in his hand.

"Why not?" Justin asked. "Why don't you just vacuum them up? It would be a lot faster than doing it this way."

"Ladybugs are good insects. They eat aphids, and aphids are bad. Aphids eat the leaves off the flowers and vegetables in the garden. We need ladybugs. The problem is that we also need happy guests."

"Can't you explain to the guests what good bugs these are?" I asked. "Ladybugs don't sting or bite or anything."

"You try talking about bugs to someone spending money here," the woman said.

So Justin and I each took a drinking glass from the bathroom and put all the ladybugs we caught inside. We must have found a hundred each, and there were still more.

"What should we do with them now?" I asked.

"Take them outdoors. Walk a good distance off. Maybe they'll fly someplace else," the woman said. But as we were about to leave the room, she stopped us. "Wait a minute," she called. "What were you fellows doing here anyway?"

"Oh," said Justin, smiling innocently and sounding more relaxed than when we were first discovered in the room, "we were looking for the owner of this place. Is it you?"

The woman laughed. "Fat chance!" she said. "You want Mr. Grinold. You certainly wouldn't find him coming to make the bed in one of the guest rooms or running around collecting bugs either, for that matter. He might be in the dining area. Or he could be in the living room. What do you want with him?" she asked suspiciously.

Justin pointed to me, and I held out the handful of flyers that I'd dropped on the bed when I started going after the ladybugs. "I wanted to ask him if he could leave these around. Maybe some of the guests would be interested," I said.

The woman took one of the flyers and read it. "Is this your mom?" she asked me.

I nodded my head.

"I've seen her and her llamas a couple of times. It looks like fun," the woman said. "What's your name?" she asked.

"Adam Fine, and this is Justin Rice," I answered. We were in this together, so she'd better know Justin's name as well as mine.

"Well, go downstairs if you want to find Mr. Grinold," the woman said. "I'm Sally Ames, and I came in here to straighten up."

"Say, Sally," said Justin, talking to her as if she were a kid our age, "we heard that there are ghosts in this place. Have you ever seen any?"

"Ghosts? Do you think I'd work in a place that was haunted?" Sally Ames asked him with a smile. "No ghosts. Just guests. And ladybugs," she answered.

"You mean, you've never seen or heard anything a little bit strange? Like doors closing or windows banging shut all on their own?"

The chambermaid looked at us for a moment as if she were deciding how to answer. "I haven't seen anything," she said slowly, "but I've heard a few stories."

"Like what?" asked Justin.

"One of the waitresses said that someone pushed her arm when she was pouring the coffee one morning. But there was no one in the pantry at the time. Someone else said maybe the ghost of the old lady who used to live here pushed her."

"You mean Mrs. Brown?" I asked.

Sally Ames nodded. "Personally I think she was just careless and was looking for someone else to blame for getting coffee all over the floor," she said.

"Anything else?" asked Justin.

"Not that I can think of," Sally said. She pulled the blanket off the bed and began straightening the sheets.

"What was the name of the waitress?" asked Justin.

Sally turned to Justin. "I think it was Dale. She was one of those college kids who came to work during the summer. She left just before Labor Day."

I saw the disappointed look on Justin's face.

He'd been all set for us to march into the dining room and interview Dale.

"Look, kids, you'd better get on downstairs. I've got twenty beds to make this morning. To say nothing of all the bathrooms that need cleaning."

"Well, thanks a lot," I said.

"Yeah," Justin said.

The two of us went downstairs. It was quiet now, though the breakfast odors were still in the air. We walked around. I had the flyers under my arm and my hand over the top of the water glass to keep the ladybugs from getting out. But even though we looked all over, we didn't see anyone.

"This is like a ghost town," said Justin.

It was a little eerie. All the guests had disappeared, and there was no sign of any waiter or waitress or hotel owner about. Justin wanted to keep opening doors and looking for clues. But I was ready to go. After all, according to what I'd seen on TV, what he wanted us to do might be considered breaking and entering, and that was a criminal offense.

"You're wrong," Justin replied when I mentioned it to him. "The door was open. We're not breaking it down or poking at locks or anything."

"Well, your dad's a lawyer, and he could defend *you* if we get into trouble," I said. "I don't have a lawyer to help me out."

"Stop worrying," Justin said. "For someone who doesn't believe in ghosts, you sure sound very nervous to me."

"There are other things to worry about besides ghosts," I said, eager to get out of the place. I tried to think of something to distract Justin.

"What we should do is go to the public library," I suggested. "Maybe we could find a book about this place and learn more about Mrs. Brown. Stuff like that."

"You know, that's not a bad idea," Justin said.

But first Justin and I went outside and walked toward the vegetable garden. We propped the glasses against some dried-up cornstalks and watched the ladybugs begin their escape.

It was only when I bent to open my bike lock that I realized I was still holding all those yellow flyers. I stuffed them back into the saddlebag. Maybe I could drop them off at the library, I thought.

There Is a Ghost!

We rode down the hill and through town to the public library. When we arrived, no one was there except Ms. Walsh, the librarian. She greeted us with a big smile. Our town library is pretty small compared with the one in Brattleboro. But usually it can come up with some sort of information to help you with whatever homework assignment you have.

"Do you just sit around and read when the library's empty?" I asked Ms. Walsh.

She laughed. "Everyone thinks that's all librarians do," she said. "We have to order new books and balance the budget, plan programs, and check that the plumbing and heating don't break down too."

"Wow," I said, "I didn't know that."

"Librarians are expected to know all sorts of things—even architecture. Have you ever seen a blueprint?" Ms. Walsh asked us. She slid some huge sheets of paper with blue lines and letters toward Justin and me. "This is the plan for the library renovation and expansion."

"What kind of renovation?" I asked, looking around the small room.

"We're going to make the whole basement into a children's area and get new shelving and furniture and lighting, and there will be a small addition put up in the back that won't change the front of the building. From the outside we'll look just as always, but inside, you won't recognize us at all. We'll be able to add a couple of thousand new books to the collection too."

"Great," said Justin. "I've already read everything you've got here."

"I doubt it," said Ms. Walsh. "There must be one or two books that are still waiting for your attention."

Justin grinned. "Not about ghosts," he said.

"That's why we came," I explained to Ms. Walsh. "We wondered if there were any history books about this town. Justin heard that there's a ghost up at the White House. Do you know any-thing about that?"

"As a matter of fact, I have exactly the book you want," said Ms. Walsh. She got out from behind her desk, took a few steps, and from a shelf in front of her picked one book out. "Here," she said, "page thirty-eight."

"Do you know *all* these books by heart?" I asked, very impressed.

"No. Just the few that I get asked about the most. I can tell you the page to find the chocolate cream pie recipe in the *Joy of Cooking*. And the weather pages in the *Farmer's Almanac*. And a couple of others." Ms. Walsh turned to Justin. "I'm surprised someone like you, who's interested in ghosts, hasn't already discovered *this* book about New England."

Justin was busy turning pages of *Green Mountain Ghosts, Ghouls & Unsolved Mysteries,* by Joseph A. Citro. "Look! Here it is," he said, pointing to the page we were looking for.

We sat down at one of the library tables and began reading. Believe it or not, there was a chapter about the White House Inn. According to the book, a guest whose last name was Brown was awakened in the night. She discovered a white-haired woman sitting in a chair near her bed. The white-haired woman told the guest that she didn't

mind her staying there but that one Mrs. Brown in the room was enough.

"See," Justin said. "I told you there was a ghost at the inn."

I turned the page. There we found mention of a chambermaid named Kelly Brown who was cleaning in one of the bedrooms when the doors began opening and closing. The chambermaid said there was no wind to explain what was happening to the doors.

"It looks like the ghost of Clara Brown shows up only to people who have the last name of Brown," I commented jokingly.

Justin took my words seriously. "No wonder we didn't see anything," he said. "Clara Brown doesn't care about two kids named Justin Rice and Adam Fine." He paused a moment, and I knew he had the same thought that I suddenly had.

"Alana Brown!" he said, referring to our new classmate.

I just knew what he was going to say next.

"We've got to get Alana to go to the White House with us. Then we'll see the ghost."

"Can we take this book out?" I asked Ms. Walsh.

"That's the reference copy," she said, looking up from her papers. "The circulating one is out. But if you have thirty cents on you, you could

31

photocopy the pages you're interested in."

I shook my head. Justin didn't have any money either.

"Okay. You can owe me the thirty cents," Ms. Walsh said.

Justin took the book over to the machine in the corner and copied the three pages that told about the White House Inn. There's a little cardboard box near the machine and people just put the ten-cents-a-page fee inside. It's done on the honor system, just like the overdue fines.

"Thanks a lot," I said to Ms. Walsh. "We'll bring the money tomorrow."

"The library is closed on Sunday," Ms. Walsh reminded us. "But don't worry. Your credit is good," she added. "Bring it the next time you come."

Justin was ready to leave, but I stopped to look again at the plans for the renovated library. I'd never seen an actual blueprint before.

"Are you going to have a party or something to celebrate?" I asked, remembering the party we had in town when the new playground was opened.

"I've been thinking about that very thing," Ms. Walsh said. "But I haven't figured out what I could do to make it special."

"How about a costume party?" Justin suggested. "I'll come as a ghost."

"If it's a costume party, people should dress up like book characters," I said.

"Ghosts are in books!" Justin shouted out, holding up the newly photocopied pages as proof. "Everything is in books," he added.

"A costume party is a great idea," Ms. Walsh said. "I don't know why I didn't think of that myself."

I wished it were me and not Justin who had come up with that idea. Suddenly I thought of something else. "How would you like to have our llamas come to the library?" I asked.

"A llama in the library! What a funny idea!" Ms. Walsh said.

"You can't have a llama in the library. What about the poop on the carpet?" Justin asked.

"Llamas are very clean," I protested. "I bet Ethan Allen and Ira Allen would never mess up your carpeting. And if they did, my dad would know how to clean it up."

"I'm afraid not, Adam. The idea of a llama in the library sounds pretty spectacular. But I shudder to think of the chaos it could cause."

"You say that only because you haven't met my llamas," I said.

Ms. Walsh shrugged. "It's sweet of you to make the offer," she said, "but I'm afraid I have to turn you down. I think I'll go with a costume affair, however. That was a great idea, Justin."

Justin beamed at Ms. Walsh's praise.

"In fact," Ms. Walsh added, "forget the thirty cents you owe me. I'll pay your copying charge myself. It's a cheap price for such a great suggestion."

I could barely stand to look at Justin's widening smile of pride.

Ms. Walsh turned to help some people who had just walked in, and we started to leave. "Good-bye!" I called out.

"Thanks again for everything," she responded.

"Come on. We've got to find Alana Brown," Justin said as we got on our bikes. Talking about the grand reopening of the library and thinking of bringing our llamas, I'd temporarily forgotten about the ghost up in the White House. But Justin hadn't. He was really obsessed about it. I had to admit, though, that this business of ghost hunting seemed a lot more interesting with Alana Brown in the picture.

5
Alana Brown

As it turned out, neither Justin nor I had the slightest idea where our new classmate lived, so we had to wait until Monday morning to confront her at school. I was curious about what it was Justin was planning to say to Alana. Did he think she'd come to the White House with us? If she did, what did he expect to happen then?

There must have been some sort of bug, other than a ladybug, going around at school because Alana was absent on Monday, and so were three other fifth graders. I thought Justin would explode with impatience when Alana was still out on Tuesday and Wednesday. But finally on Thursday she was back in school. At lunchtime that day Justin grabbed me by the shirtsleeve and pulled me over toward her. I was glad to have an excuse to get near her. She was wearing a bright blue shirt that made her eyes look bluer than I'd ever seen them. But the ghost stuff really embarrassed me. This whole thing was Justin's idea, so I mumbled to him that he'd have to do the talking.

He invited Alana to come with us after school to the White House.

"Why do you want to go there?" Alana asked. She looked puzzled, and I couldn't blame her.

"Well, it used to be owned by a woman named Brown," Justin answered. We hadn't discussed how much of the story we should tell Alana, but Justin must have realized that it didn't make sense unless she heard it all. "Some people say she haunts the place. But it seems as if the only people who have really seen the ghost are people named Brown."

"Is this some sort of trick you want to play on me?" Alana asked suspiciously.

"No. Honest," I chimed in. "Do you have the pages we copied at the library?" I looked at Justin.

He pulled them out of his pocket. By now they were very rumpled but still readable. Alana studied them.

"This is weird," she said.

"It is," I said. "I don't believe in ghosts. If you came with us to the White House, maybe we could prove once and for all to Justin that there's nothing to this story."

"Or maybe we'll prove that the place really is haunted," Justin said hopefully.

Alana shook her head, and her long braid swung from side to side. "It sure sounds nuts to me. But I'll meet you," she said. "Only I can't go until Saturday morning. Is that okay with you?"

Justin sighed impatiently. But I said, "If the ghost has been there this long, what's another couple of days?"

"I guess you're right," Justin said. "What time's good for you?"

"Ten o'clock," Alana answered.

"Great!" said Justin.

We said we'd meet outside on the inn's front porch.

I was amazed at what a good sport Alana was, agreeing to go with us on that wild-goose chase, or should I say wild-*ghost* chase? No wonder I liked her, I thought.

The only problem was that around nine o'clock on Saturday morning, the phone rang. It was Justin. I could hardly recognize his voice. He had caught the class bug, and he sounded really sick. "My mom won't let me out of the house," he said. "I got a temperature and a sore throat. Let's go next week instead," he croaked before he hung up.

"What about Alana?" I asked, but it was too late. He couldn't hear me. Now I was stuck. I couldn't even call Alana to postpone the meeting. I still didn't know her address or her phone number or even her parents' first names. I opened the phone book and counted thirty-seven Browns. I'd never known there were so many around here.

So it looked as if I had no choice. But though I felt sorry for Justin, in a way I was pleased. It wouldn't be so terrible to be alone with Alana.

At ten o'clock I was locking up my bike in the parking lot of the White House Inn.

There were a couple of dark clouds above and a cold wind up on the hill this morning. I can remember more than one year when we've had several inches of snow in October. Maybe this year we'd even get snow in September, I thought as I walked through the parking lot. I studied the license plates of the parked cars: North Carolina, Florida, Connecticut, New York, New Jersey. I saw a great bumper sticker that my mom would get a kick out of: FLEECE ON EARTH, GOOD WOOL TO EWE.

"Hi," a voice called out. "Where's your shadow?"

Because I was still wearing my biking helmet, I didn't hear her very well at first. But then I turned around and saw Alana getting off her bike.

"What did you say about shadows?" I asked, confused.

"Justin. I always see the two of you together," she explained.

"He's home sick. He wants us to wait until next week."

"Why wait?" Alana asked me. "We don't need him, do we? If we find a ghost, we'll tell him all about it," she said.

I stared at her. She was really beautiful, I thought. Besides her long golden braid and the bluest eyes I'd ever seen, I really liked her smile. One of her front teeth was a little chipped, but it just made the smile seem bigger.

At that moment I was very glad that Justin wasn't there. "Okay," I said. "Let's go."

I was acting as if I knew what I was doing, but really I had no plan at all. We walked up the steps of the inn, and I could already smell the fire going in the fireplace. If I hadn't been feeling nervous about walking into the inn, it would have felt good to be going inside, out of the wind.

"Wow. This is some place," Alana commented. "How would you like to live here?"

"It's hard to imagine that it used to be a home for one family," I responded.

Before I had time to think which way to go, a man appeared, walking toward the front entranceway. He stopped when he saw us.

"Are you kids looking for someone?" he asked.

I could hear the distant tinkle of china, and once again I could smell the coffee and other breakfast smells. For a moment I paused, not knowing what to say to him. "Well, not exactly looking for someone . . . ," I stammered. "That is, I saw a book in the library that says there was a ghost in this place. Have you ever seen it?"

The man smiled. "I've seen that book, but I've never been able to spot the ghost. In fact I keep a copy of the book in our sitting room for the guests to read."

He held out his hand to us as if we were adults. "I'm Mr. Grinold. I own this place."

I shook his hand. "Doesn't it scare them knowing that your place might be haunted?" I asked.

"No one's ever checked out with a complaint," said Mr. Grinold. "In fact I think some people sit up nights hoping for a sighting." He paused a moment. "What's your name?" he asked.

"Adam Fine, and this is Alana Brown." Alana nodded in greeting.

"Ah. Brown," the man said, smiling again.

"Yeah," I said. "After reading about the ghost appearing only to people named Brown, we thought we should test it out."

"Why not?" asked Mr. Grinold. "You ought to start with the secret stairway."

"Secret stairway?" both Alana and I echoed.

The man smiled and nodded. "Come along," he said. "I'll show you."

Justin would *really* have something to feel sick about when he heard that he'd missed seeing the secret stairway at the White House, I thought.

We followed Mr. Grinold into one of the dining rooms that weren't being used that morning. He opened a door of what looked like an ordinary china cabinet. Then he pressed a hidden latch, and suddenly he was able to move the entire cabinet to reveal that it was really a door. Behind it was a stairway.

"You can walk right on up to the top," Mr. Grinold told us. "Turn left, and you'll find another door. When you open it, you'll be on the second floor."

"Why did they build this?" I asked, looking up at the dimly lit stairwell.

"Was it part of the Underground Railroad?" Alana asked. I thought that was a really smart question and wished I'd asked it. At school we'd learned that there were houses with secret doors

and secret rooms where escaping slaves could hide, back in the days before the Civil War.

"No," Mr. Grinold said. "I wish I could pretend the stairway had such an important purpose. I think when the house was being designed at the beginning of the twentieth century, the owner or the architect had a sense of humor and thought it would be fun to add this feature. I suppose the servants might have used it to get from one floor to another and to keep out of sight."

Alana started up the stairs, and I followed her. The dining room light lit our way. But as we got farther from it, it became more difficult to see.

"I wish I had a flashlight," I muttered to Alana as I bumped into her.

"I see a little light ahead. It must be coming from the doorway that will let us out," Alana told me.

We climbed a few more steps, and then she found the doorknob of the exit. We could see the second-floor landing in front of us. We closed the door behind us, and when we looked back, it appeared to be just an ordinary closet door. Then we raced down the main stairway to the ground floor.

Mr. Grinold was waiting for us there. "Well," he asked us, "did you see any ghosts?"

To tell the truth, I'd been so impressed by that

staircase that I'd forgotten I was supposed to be looking for a ghost.

"Maybe it's their day off," said Alana with a grin.

"As long as you're here, you're welcome to look in one of the rooms too," Mr. Grinold offered. "Go up to room nine," he said. "It's on the second floor. The door's open, and no one is staying there at the moment."

"Gee, thanks!" I said, thrilled that this was working out so easily. Too bad Justin wasn't here. After all, it had been his idea.

Alana and I slowly mounted the steep staircase in the center hall. Room 9 was at the end of the hall on the second floor. The door was closed, but when I turned the knob, it opened easily.

"I'll turn on the light," said Alana, moving toward an oak dresser with a lamp on it.

"Ghosts probably prefer the dark," I said, but it was a dark day and I was glad to have the light on.

Now I could see that the double bed was covered with a quilt of blue and green fabric. The carpeting was pale blue.

"It looks more cozy than spooky," I commented. I walked over to a door and peeked inside. It was the bathroom. There were no ghosts in there using the facilities.

"This must be a closet," said Alana, opening another door. Suddenly she let out a little shriek.

"What is it?" I asked, rushing toward her.

Alana giggled. "This fell on my head," she said, picking up an extra pillow that had been resting on an overhead shelf in the closet.

"Do you suppose someone pushed it down?" I asked incredulously.

"You mean, the ghost of Mrs. Brown?" asked Alana softly.

"Well, I don't believe in ghosts. But it is a strange coincidence that the pillow fell on you."

At that moment the light went out. Alana reached out and grabbed my hand.

I held on, glad not to be alone in the room. The cozy bedroom had turned spooky after all. "Maybe the bulb burned out," I whispered hopefully.

"Are you scared?" asked Alana.

"No," I lied, giving her hand a squeeze. I still didn't believe in ghosts, but I admit I was feeling a bit shaky. Without letting go of Alana's hand, I walked toward the bathroom. I tried to turn on the light, but nothing happened.

"Mrs. Brown, are you here?" Alana asked, looking up toward the ceiling.

Of course there was no answer.

"You don't have to worry. I'm not going to

stay. I just came to admire your old house," Alana told the darkness.

I sniffed the air. I remember once reading something about how you can smell a ghost. An old woman like Mrs. Brown would have worn some sort of flowery perfume. To my horror, there was a sweet scent in the air.

"I think we should get out of here," I said to Alana.

"That's fine with me," she agreed.

We left the room and hurried back down the stairs. There were a few people in the front room now, and a couple of them were carrying flashlights and candles. Though it was not yet ten-thirty in the morning, the room was dark. It was dark outside too.

"Look what you did," I teased Alana, and she giggled nervously. We both felt relieved to be surrounded by other people and not alone upstairs in room 9.

"Looks like we're going to get a storm," I said.

"We'd better hurry home," Alana replied.

"We seem to have lost power," Mr. Grinold was explaining to his guests. "I hope all will be in order before it's time to start cooking dinner."

I nodded good-bye to the owner of the White House, but he was so busy talking that I'm not sure he even noticed us. As we left the building, I realized that I was still holding Alana's hand. "Thanks for being such a good sport," I said, letting go.

"Why not?" Alana said. "It was fun. Especially now that we're out of that room."

"Maybe someday you can come over to my house," I said to her. "We have two llamas in my family. I bet you'd like them."

"Neat," Alana said. "Someone told me you had llamas. I'd love to see them."

I unlocked my bike and put my helmet on my head. "Don't you wear a helmet when you ride?" I asked her.

She shook her head. "I hate the feel of my helmet, so I hardly ever wear it. Only when my father's watching. He makes a big deal of it."

"He's right," I said as I mounted my bike. "It's better to be safe than sorry." Boy, I thought, that was dumb of me. I sounded just like a teacher or a parent.

"So long," Alana shouted, and she was off down the hill. I watched her go. Even under the darkening skies, I could see her golden braid flying out behind her as she rode. At the foot of the hill Alana made a left. My route took me to the right. Why didn't I invite her home with me *today?* I wondered. Well, it was too late now. But I definitely would invite her another day soon. I felt the first drop of rain on my hand, and I knew that there would be a lot more to follow. Luckily I made it home before the real downpour began.

We didn't have any electrical power at my house either. I guessed the wind must have brought a tree down onto a power line. The telephone lines weren't affected, however. So after I changed into a dry pair of jeans, I called Justin. Even if he was feeling sick, I knew he'd want to know the details of Alana's and my visit to the White House. Wait till he heard about the secret staircase!

6
The Accident

Justin's line was busy. After a couple of unsuccessful tries I went into the kitchen to see if there was any lunch. But it was an automatic move on the part of my legs. It wasn't as if they were getting an urgent message from my stomach. I wasn't really hungry at all. In fact I was feeling kind of achy.

My mother felt my forehead with her hand and announced that beyond a doubt I had a fever. It was too dark in the house, without electricity, to take my temperature with a thermometer. We would never have been able to read it.

"It must be from being out in that rain," I told

her as I got into bed. My throat was feeling scratchy, and my eyes were burning.

"One rainstorm shouldn't make a healthy kid sick," she announced. "You did the right thing by changing your clothing, but whatever you have must have been incubating inside you already. I'll bet you caught the class bug, like Justin."

For the next day and a half, I didn't feel like getting out of bed. I slept and drank fruit juice or tea sweetened with honey and then slept again. I didn't want to watch the baseball play-offs on TV or even listen on the radio. I didn't miss the electricity and wasn't aware when it came back on fourteen hours after we'd lost it.

It wasn't until Monday morning that I began to feel like myself again. But I still wasn't well enough to go to school. I was sitting at the kitchen table, drinking a cup of hot cocoa and looking at the sports page in the newspaper. When I turned the paper over to the other side, my heart did a somersault.

The headline read GIRL BIKER HIT BY CAR ON SATURDAY DIES. I thought immediately of Alana. I remembered seeing her ride off in the rain. I scanned the story underneath the headline, but I was so nervous that I could hardly make out the letters. I forced myself to start again at the top and read slowly, word by word.

•••

On Saturday, in the midst of a heavy rainstorm and winds that caused power outages for 20 miles, a young woman riding a bike was sideswiped at the intersection of routes 100 and 9 in Wilmington by a pickup truck. The driver of the pickup was Doug Poole, age 38, of Marlboro. The traffic light was out, and Poole admits he drove through the Wilmington intersection at about 40 miles an hour.

"I didn't see her," the anguished Poole told police who arrived at the scene. "I had no visibility at all, even though my wipers were going at their fastest speed."

The young woman, who was not wearing a helmet, probably skidded into Poole's truck because of the wet road. She was taken to Memorial Hospital, where she was in a coma for 36 hours before her death from brain injuries. Police are withholding her name until her family has been notified.

Poole agreed to take an alcohol test and was found not to have been intoxicated. "This was an unavoidable accident," Police Chief Ron Cole announced. "The lack of electricity, the unusual darkness because of the storm, and the heavy rain all contributed to

this tragedy." It is speculated that had the bike rider been wearing a helmet, the fatality might not have occurred.

I sat at the table and read the article a second and a third time. I didn't believe in ghosts, yet somehow a ghost had gotten Alana. And it was my fault. She would never have ridden to and from the White House if it hadn't been for me.

I discovered that tears were dripping down my face. I hardly even knew Alana. She'd been in my class for only a few weeks, and except for the short time we spent together on Saturday morning, she was practically a stranger. Still, I thought about her beautiful golden braid and the good soapy smell when I stood next to her. I remembered her chipped front tooth and how it made her smile seem even bigger and happier. I remembered how she gasped when the pillow fell out of the closet. We both had laughed, I thought. Now I'd never see her or laugh with her again.

My mother came into the room. "Adam," she said, "you look terrible. I thought you were getting better."

"It's not my throat," I croaked to her. "Look at this." I held out the paper.

My mother nodded. "I read that story already. It's a real tragedy," she said. "It's why Dad and I always insist you wear a helmet when you ride your bike."

"She was in my class," I told her.

"She was?" my mom asked in a puzzled voice. "I didn't remember that the article gave her name and age."

"It doesn't. But I know anyhow. I was with her on Saturday when it began to rain. I even told her she should wear a helmet," I said. As I said it, I shuddered with a thought. Why hadn't I lent her mine? Maybe then she would still be alive.

"Adam, you may be wrong," my mother said. "Maybe it isn't your classmate."

I shook my head. I just knew.

Later in the day, when school was over, I phoned Justin. I was hoping he'd tell me that by some miracle Alana had been in class. I tried to sound casual when I spoke to him, as if I'd known nothing about the accident. "Did Alana tell you about the White House?" I asked him after he gave me our math homework.

"Naw. She wasn't in school today," he said. So then I knew for sure. Alana was dead.

I was well enough to go outdoors, so I went to the shed where our llamas are kept. I put my arm around Ethan Allen. Justin thinks he's my best friend, but there are some things I can tell our llama that I would never tell Justin. Only this time

I didn't even say anything. I just began crying. Ethan Allen didn't move. He stood still and let me wipe my eyes on his soft coat.

Ira Allen moved close to me too. It was as if he were trying to let me know that he cared about how I felt also. "I was going to bring Alana to meet you both," I sobbed. "You'd have liked her. I liked her a lot."

I didn't go back into the house until I stopped crying. When I did, I ran straight upstairs to the bathroom and washed my face so my parents and April wouldn't guess.

The next day Mom said I was well enough to return to school. It was raining, so I took the bus instead of riding my bike. I joked with some of the other kids, but at the same time I was dreading the moment I'd first see Alana's empty chair in the classroom.

I tried not to look at the seat where Alana had sat, but my head kept turning in that direction. She'd sat to the left, two rows ahead of me, so it was hard not to notice.

Mrs. Wurst called us to attention. "By now most of you have heard about the tragic accident that occurred on Saturday," she said.

We all nodded, and there was a mumble of voices. "You'll notice an empty chair in our class," she continued. "Chad Embers will probably be out for the rest of the week. His sister's funeral is on Friday morning. She didn't have any identification on her, and her parents thought she was visiting a friend. So the family didn't even know that it was Diane Embers who had been killed until she didn't return home from school yesterday.

"Those of you who want to show support for Chad and his family by attending the funeral should get your parents' permission, and we'll go directly from school on Friday. You'll need to dress appropriately. No T-shirts. The boys don't need to wear neckties, but if you do, it would be an added sign of respect for the deceased."

"I don't even have a tie," one of the boys across the room said.

But I wasn't thinking about ties. Chad's sister? Chad's been in my class since kindergarten. His older sister was in high school now. She used to bring Chad to school when he was little, but I hadn't seen her around in ages.

Chad's sister was dead. But that must mean Alana was alive. So where was she?

"Where's Alana?" I called out.

Mrs. Wurst looked at me, surprised. I'm not one of those kids who call things out in class. "Alana's had a relapse. It's that forty-eight-hour flu again. The one that's been through this class and knocked you out for a couple of days," she said.

I couldn't help myself. An enormous smile came across my face. Alana was alive. The ghost hadn't gotten her. The car hadn't hit her. She was alive.

I'm sure my classmates must have thought there was something weird about my reaction. I shouldn't have been smiling at the news that a classmate was sick. But what's a forty-eight-hour flu compared with being hit by a car? Nothing. It's a mosquito bite compared with chicken pox. It's a bee sting compared with death.

I spent the rest of the day feeling very happy. It wasn't until after school, when I was brushing the llamas and telling them the good news, that I realized something that I'd overlooked. One person's good news was another person's bad news. Alana was alive, but poor Chad had lost his sister.

7
Llama Marinara

I never told Alana that for twenty-four hours I thought she was dead. But as soon as she was back in school on Wednesday, I invited her to come and meet our llamas.

"How about this Saturday?" she asked, giving me her big chipped-tooth smile. "I can't wait to visit with them."

I secretly hoped Alana would be glad to see me too.

Justin was a bit put off that Alana was coming over. Now that she'd served her purpose as ghost bait—and failed at her mission, at that—she'd become invisible to him again. But then it turned out that one of his father's clients had invited the Rice family to spend Saturday visiting his home in the Northeast Kingdom (which is actually just another part of Vermont), so Justin wasn't around when Alana came to my house.

Saturday morning I was out on the road at the edge of our property waiting for Alana. I didn't want her to get lost and just zip by on her bike. It was a perfect Indian summer day and totally different from the weather the week before. The temperature was expected to go up to the seventies, and the leaves on the trees were brilliant gold and red. I picked up a bright yellow leaf the color of Alana's braid and waited for her.

Suddenly she arrived. "Adam!" she shouted in delight. "Look what I have!"

I noticed at once that Alana was wearing her helmet, but that wasn't what she was referring to. She pointed to a pair of brightly colored ribbons with bells attached that she was wearing around her neck. "These are presents for your llamas. My parents bought them in Mexico before I was born. We found them when we were packing for our move. My father almost threw them out, but I thought they might come in handy. And I didn't even know about you or your llamas. Isn't that amazing?"

I felt like saying that the only amazing thing

was that this smiling girl had come to spend the day with me. But of course I didn't.

"Come on," I said. "I'll introduce you to our llamas. Those ribbons will look great on them when my mother takes them on one of her treks."

Alana got off her bike and pushed it along. "Is it a lot of work to take care of them?" she asked.

"Nope. They don't eat much, and they're really clean animals. Sometimes I brush their hair a little. But it's not a big deal."

"That's cool."

"I wanted to bring them to the library next spring, when they have the big opening after the renovation, but Ms. Walsh didn't believe me when I told her how clean and well behaved they are. She thinks they'll make a mess, so she turned down my offer."

"Has she seen them in person?" Alana asked.

"You mean, did I invite her over to see them?"

"Yeah. Or did you take them to visit the library?"

"No. But that's a great idea," I said excitedly. "We could do that today!"

I rushed ahead toward the llamas. "There's Ethan Allen!" I called to her as I pointed to our white-haired llama. "Ira Allen is the one that has dark brown hair. You're going to love them."

Suddenly about twenty feet away from the llamas I stopped, horrified.

"Is that what llamas smell like?" Alana asked. She was standing alongside, and like me, she could smell a strong and very unlovable odor.

"That's not llama. That's skunk!" I said. "They must have been sprayed." It had never happened before. Why did it have to happen now?

Alana put a hand up to cover her nose. "You can't bring them to the library," she said. "They'll never let you in the door."

"Just you wait and see," I said. "I'm going to clean them up." I was determined that first Alana and then Ms. Walsh would fall in love with Ethan and Ira Allen.

"Justin's dog, Matty, was sprayed by a skunk one day last spring," I told Alana. "I remember that he poured tomato juice all over her. It killed the odor."

"Sounds weird," said Alana. "But it couldn't make them smell worse than they do now."

We rushed to the house. Alana introduced herself to my mom and April while I started pulling things out of the kitchen cupboard, looking for some cans of tomato juice.

"Don't we have any tomato juice?" I asked my mother desperately.

"I don't think so," she responded. "But there's a half gallon of orange juice in the fridge. Can't you drink that?"

"It's not for drinking," I explained impatiently. "A skunk sprayed the llamas. I need the tomato juice to try to counteract the odor. Where's Dad? Can he go to Grand Union and buy some?"

"He's not home." My mother reminded me that even though my father had taken the day off from work, he'd already left the house. He was helping old Mrs. Peaslee, one of our neighbors who lived alone, by taking down her screens and putting up her storm windows.

"Isn't there anything else you could use instead of tomato juice?" Alana asked. "How about tomato sauce or ketchup or something like that?"

"Llama marinara?" my mother exclaimed. "There's got to be another alternative."

"I want to smell the llamas!" demanded April.

"You'll be sorry," I called after her as she ran out of the house and toward the animals.

"Wait a minute," I said. My eye had just landed on the bookshelves above the kitchen counter. Mostly my mother kept her cookbooks there. But there was a book called *Dear Anne and Nan* that was full of solutions for household problems. I grabbed it off the shelf. "I bet there's something in here about getting rid of skunk smell."

It took longer than it should have because I didn't use the index, as we were taught to do at school. But I still found an answer to my question.

"Do we have any wine?" I asked.

"Wine? You aren't going to give the llamas wine to drink, are you?" my mother asked. "Because if that's your plan, I won't permit it."

"No, not to drink," I said. "Wait a minute." I reread the words. "It could be wine or vinegar or anything with a five percent acid content. 'The acid cuts through the oil in which the skunk scent is suspended. Follow with a good soapy bath—'"

"They smell terrible, horrible, awful!" April shouted, running back into the house.

"You didn't believe us," Alana said to her. "We told you it was pretty bad."

A minute later we all trooped back to the llamas: April, my mother, Alana, and I. Even the cat came along. I was holding a bottle of white vinegar and a bottle of wine vinegar. After all, Anne and Nan had been writing about cleaning up a dog. Two llamas would need a lot more liquid to do the trick.

April danced around holding her nose, but Alana was a good sport and helped me rub vinegar into the llamas' hair. I don't like the smell of

skunk, but I didn't like the smell of vinegar either. The poor llamas didn't know what was going on. Ethan Allen held pretty still, but Ira kept moving away from us. Finally I had to hold him by the halter while Alana rubbed the vinegar into his hairy coat.

Then I got a bottle of dishwashing liquid and the hose, and we gave both llamas a good shampoo. We toweled them dry too. Usually, if the llamas are wet, I know that in a few hours they'll dry out in the air. But I couldn't wait for that now. I wanted to take them to the library, and I didn't think Ms. Walsh would appreciate a pair of wet llamas arriving on her doorstep.

"Get me Mom's hair dryer," I instructed April, because by now my mother had returned to the house. Then I realized that the dryer's cord wouldn't be long enough to be of any use. I turned to Alana. "There's an extension cord in the right-hand drawer under the counter in the kitchen. My mother will give it to you. I need that too."

Both girls ran off while I continued towel-drying the llamas. I knew April had enjoyed every moment of the cleanup. It was better than any Saturday morning TV cartoon show! I hoped Alana would forgive me for this smelly introduction to the llamas.

When April and Alana returned, I hooked up the hair dryer. It would have been much better if my mom had had two hair dryers. But with only one head, I guess one was all she ever thought she'd need. I blow-dried the llamas until my arms got tired. Then Alana took a turn. April begged for a turn too, so I let her.

It was only after the llamas were more or less dry that I realized how wet both Alana and I were.

"Let's go get cleaned up," I told her. "I'll lend you some dry clothes if you want too."

My mother thought we should each take a shower. So I went into the upstairs bathroom, and Alana went into the downstairs one. In a little while we were both clean and dry.

"Can I wear some of your clothes too?" April asked. She was wearing one of my old T-shirts over her own clothing as Alana and I started down the road with the llamas.

I'd explained our plan to my mom. "It will be great publicity for Fine Llama Treks," I said. "People will come from all over to attend the library opening." Then I thought of the new baby. "Will you be able to do the treks next summer?"

"I've planned it out," my mother responded. "I'm going to get a high school girl to work as a mother's helper. She'll take care of things once or twice a week when I go off for a few hours. It should all work out fine."

"Fine. Fine Llama Treks," I said. I like my last name. It's a fine one.

As Alana and I walked down the road, I explained to her about the baby that was coming in April. She was the first of my friends to hear the news from me, and after seeing the sex film two weeks before, I wondered how she'd react.

"Oh Adam!" she exclaimed. "Lucky you! April is a darling, and now you're going to have another brother or sister. My sister, Adele, is a freshman at the University of Vermont. But I've always wanted a younger sister or brother."

"You can share mine," I offered. "I can tell that April likes you a lot. And I bet the baby will too."

It was easier to say that than to tell Alana that *I* liked her. At that moment I felt great. What could be more wonderful than walking down the road with our two llamas, accompanied by Alana Brown? We'd tied the Mexican ribbons around the halters of each llama, and the bells rang as we walked. Cars passing us on the road honked their horns in greeting.

"Your llamas are wonderful," Alana said, "when they smell like llamas and not like skunks."

"I told you they were great pets."

When we arrived at the library, I didn't have a plank to help Ethan and Ira Allen up the entrance steps. So Alana went into the library and asked Ms. Walsh if she could step outside for a minute.

"My goodness!" the librarian exclaimed when she saw her two surprise visitors. "Are they looking for a good book to read?"

"Nope," I said. "They've just come by to say hello. I wanted you to see how clean and quiet llamas are."

Ms. Walsh put out her hand and petted first Ira and then Ethan Allen. She moved slowly, so neither animal backed away from her. I hoped her hand had landed on dry spots. Both llamas still had some damp patches.

Ethan Allen bobbed his head, and the bells on his ribbon jingled slightly. He began to hum softly the way llamas sometimes do.

"They *are* beautiful animals," Ms. Walsh admitted to me. "I've never been this close to one before."

A car pulled up in front of the library. "Ms. Walsh! Are those new library assistants?" a voice called out.

Ms. Walsh laughed aloud and waved her hand. "That's Mr. Jordan. He's the president of the library board," she told Alana and me.

"They're auditioning to appear at the grand

reopening after the renovation," I announced to Mr. Jordan after he got out of his car and came toward us.

"Well, sign them up at once," the library board president said. "You won't find anything more eye-catching than those two llamas. Unless someone around here owns an elephant," he added.

"I'll check out the elephant population of Wilmington," Ms. Walsh agreed. "But, Adam, just in case none turns up, I'd like to accept your offer of bringing the llamas to the opening."

"It's a deal!" I said, holding out my hand. We shook on it.

And it was all because of Alana's suggestion— and despite the early-morning visit from that skunk.

Ghosts on Toast

Somehow, after my mini-adventure in the dark with Alana at the White House, I thought we were finished hunting for ghosts. I'd found something far better than a ghost—a new friend. And as my mom's pregnancy progressed, I was busy at home helping her out with chores. Things like getting the old newspapers tied up and the bottles and cans taken out to the garage so everything was ready for my dad's weekly trips to the dump (or I should say, "transfer station"—that's what we call the dump now). I also helped unload and put away groceries when Mom went shopping. So between schoolwork, homework, household chores, taking care of the llamas, and playing with April, who had recently learned how to play checkers, ghosts were not something I had much time to think about.

But then Alana came to school waving a coupon she'd cut out of the *Valley News*.

"Look at this," she said to Justin and me. "With this little piece of paper and a ten-dollar bill, we can get dinner at the White House."

I examined the coupon and read the small print on it, something Alana had apparently forgotten to do.

"With this little piece of paper, *one* person can get dinner at the White House, and only on Sunday evenings," I told her.

"That's okay," replied Alana. "You probably both have copies of the paper at your houses. Just cut out the coupons and we'll all go. I want to sit in that fancy dining room and eat a meal."

"That's a great idea!" said Justin, who never misses a chance to eat another meal. But he tried to cover his enthusiasm for food by saying, "I've been wanting to study that hidden staircase you said was behind the china cabinet in the back dining room. Maybe this time the ghost will finally appear."

71

"Come off it, Justin," I said. "You know as well as I do that there isn't a ghost. Haven't you gotten that through your head yet?"

"Alana and I will go without you if you aren't interested," said Justin. But of course I was glad of an excuse to spend more time with Alana, so I agreed to join them for Sunday dinner. So that's how Justin, Alana, and I, all wearing our best clothes, went to the White House on a Sunday evening. I hardly recognized Alana. Instead of a braid, her hair hung loose all around her head. She was wearing a dark green corduroy dress. I'd never seen her in anything except jeans before. She really looked awesome. It made me feel good that I'd come along with her and Justin.

Justin's father drove us to the inn, and my father had agreed to pick us up an hour and a half later. "Are you waiting for your parents?" the waiter asked us when we stood hesitantly in the doorway of the dining room.

"No, it's just us," Alana said.

The waiter raised his eyebrows but said nothing. He picked up three large menus and motioned for us to follow as he led the way to a table.

It felt strange to be sitting in that elegant room with my friends. There were six tables in the room, set with white linen cloths and napkins arranged in a fancy way at each place. There were crystal goblets and gleaming silverware. It wasn't exactly the way it looks when we sit down to supper at home.

I picked up the large cloth napkin that was at my place and opened it on my lap. No elbows on the table, I reminded myself as I sat up straight and looked around. There were only two other tables occupied. An elderly couple sat off to one side, and a couple around the age of my parents were at another table. My mother had said Sunday was probably a slow time, and that was why the coupon was in the paper to encourage guests. I dug into my pocket and took out the coupon. Justin and Alana did the same. Then we all opened our menus.

"What are you going to have?" Justin asked.

I knew my mother was making hamburgers at home, but there were no hamburgers on this menu. Most of the dishes had foreign-sounding names like Filet of Sole Amandine, Pasta Primavera, Chicken Provencal, Veal Marsala, Duck à l'Orange. I picked Chicken Livers Madeira, which was served with "toast points." My grandmother used to cook chicken livers whenever we went to visit her, and I hadn't eaten any in ages.

"Yuck!" exclaimed Justin. Like dandelion jelly,

chicken livers didn't appeal to him.

The waiter came over to us. He picked up the discount coupons. "The ten-dollar dinner includes only an entrée. Soup, salad, and dessert are extra. And of course drinks are extra too."

"No Cokes." Justin sighed. He took a sip of his water.

"Rats," I said.

"No rats on the menu tonight," the waiter said seriously. But when I looked at his face, I could see he was smiling.

We ordered our entrées. Alana selected the chicken, and Justin picked the duck. Then we sat waiting for our food and feeling a little bit sheepish.

I turned my head and looked over at the other diners. "No ghost tonight," I told Justin.

"Not yet," he said. "But you wait. I'm not giving up." With that he got up from the table and left Alana and me.

"Where do you think he went?" I asked Alana as I leaned over and picked up Justin's napkin, which had fallen from his lap and landed on the floor.

She shrugged. "The john?" she said.

But when ten minutes passed and Justin hadn't returned, I got up from the table. "I'm going to look for him," I told Alana. "Maybe he's sick."

I followed a sign that pointed to the men's room. I called out his name, but there was no answer, and I didn't see him anywhere.

Hesitantly I opened the door to the one cubicle. It was empty.

I left the rest room, and as I started back to our table, I remembered that Justin had said he wanted to investigate the secret staircase. I went into the back dining room that hid the entrance to the staircase. There were no guests eating in the room, so the light wasn't on. The cabinet was in place, and it seemed impossible that Justin could have gone up the stairs. Unless he had remembered my description of how the stairway led up to the second floor and had gone upstairs to find it from that direction.

Quickly I ran to the main entrance of the inn and hurried up the stairs. There were many doors on the second floor, and I couldn't recall which door was the exit to the stairway. There was no one around I could ask. I opened the nearest unmarked door. It was a linen closet full of sheets. I closed it and moved on, looking for the next unmarked door, which turned out to be a closet full of cleaning tools. I was really beginning to feel silly. Justin was probably downstairs eating his supper with Alana. I decided to open just one more and then go back downstairs.

I opened a door, to a room that contained a sink. That's it, I thought. I'm going downstairs. But just at that moment I heard a muffled cry. I ran along the hallway listening. I didn't believe in ghosts, but I couldn't see anyone or anything that could be making those sounds or the accompanying thumps that I now heard too. I moved down the hallway and found myself in front of still another door. I admit I was a little scared, but I took a deep breath and pulled the door open.

A disheveled Justin was standing there.

"Where were you?" he asked accusingly.

"Where was I? I was looking for you. What happened?"

"I found this entrance to the secret stairs, and just as I was walking down them, the ghost shut the door behind me. I was on the stairs in the middle between the two doors, and it was totally dark with the door closed. I made my way downstairs, but I couldn't get the cabinet to open. And when I got upstairs, I couldn't get *this* door to open either."

"I don't think it was the ghost who shut the door," I said to him. "I bet one of the chambermaids walked by and gave the door a good slam. They don't want any of their guests going in here in the dark. Someone could fall and get hurt."

"It was a ghost," Justin insisted.

"You do look kind of pale, like you'd actually seen a ghost. But that's probably because you were scared of spending the night in the dark stairway."

"If I'm pale, it's because I'm hungry," Justin protested. "Let's go eat."

I thought of Alana sitting alone at the table wondering what had happened to us. We hurried back down the stairs and into the dining area. Sure enough, there was Alana eating her dinner, and Justin's and my food waiting at our empty places.

"I decided to begin without you," Alana said.

"That was smart," I replied. "Ten dollars is a lot of money to pay for cold food." The food on my plate was arranged in a pattern with the triangles of toast pointing to the food in the center of the dish. It looked like an advertisement in one of my mother's magazines. However, my cold chicken livers didn't taste at all the way my grandmother prepared them.

"Not ten dollars. Eleven fifty," Alana corrected me. Our parents had said that even if the meal cost ten dollars, we had to leave a 15 percent tip for the waiter. Luckily all our parents had been so amused at the thought of their fifth-grade kids eating at this place that they had offered to pay for the meals. "It can't hurt to learn about gracious living," my dad had said as he gave me the eleven dollars and fifty cents. "Don't forget to use your best manners so you don't embarrass your mother and me."

I guessed that meant I'd have to eat everything on my plate. There was a pile of mashed squash, some rice, and a few baby string beans. They all were cold. I turned to Justin. His food was probably just as cold as mine, but nothing discourages his appetite.

"This duck is great," he said. "My mother never makes it."

I picked up one of the toast points. Cold toast in a restaurant tastes just like cold toast at home.

"Don't you like the squash?" Justin asked when he saw the pale orange mound still on my plate.

I shook my head.

"I'll eat it," he offered. A moment later it had disappeared.

As we finished our meal, the waiter came over to us. "Was everything satisfactory?" he asked. It wasn't his fault that my food was cold, so I didn't say anything.

"It was great," said Alana, smiling at him.

The waiter smiled back at all of us. "I have some good news for you," he said. "Mr. Grinold told me that he's going to throw in free desserts for all of you. I'll bring the dessert tray to the table," he added as he removed our empty plates.

"Free dessert!" said Justin, smiling proudly as if he'd arranged the whole thing.

"Look at that!" exclaimed Alana.

We turned to see that the waiter was pushing a cart toward our table, and on it were *eight* different desserts.

"Let me tell you what's here," the waiter said. There was chocolate mousse cake, cheesecake, apple pie, pecan pie, key lime pie, and some other things that I've forgotten.

"Oh, boy," said Justin.

"Waiter," called the elderly man at the table across the room.

"Take your pick," said the waiter, winking at us. "I'd better go see what that gentleman wants."

"First dibs on the pecan pie," said Justin.

"Hey, ladies first," I responded. "Alana should get first pick."

"She's not a lady. She's just a kid like us," said Justin.

"That's okay," said Alana. "I want the key lime pie."

I took the chocolate mousse cake. It was an excellent reward for eating those cold veggies and cold livers.

"Okay. Next I'm taking the cheesecake," said Justin.

I looked at Alana.

"I'm too full," she said. "I can't eat any more."

"You're sure?" I asked. When she nodded, I reached for a slice of apple pie with a sweet white sauce on it. After that I was too full to eat another bite. But Justin wasn't going to stop.

"I want to get our money's worth," he explained as he ate each of the remaining desserts on the tray. I noticed that he secretly had to open his belt buckle and open the button on his slacks, but he kept on going until there was nothing left on the cart.

It was an amazing feat. Alana and I watched Justin and then looked at each other in amazement. I put my hand under the table and found her hand. I gave it a squeeze, and she squeezed my hand back.

"I'm sorry I was so long," the waiter said, returning to us. "That gentleman accidentally knocked over his glass of wine onto his wife's dress and I had to get . . ." The waiter didn't finish speaking.

Justin looked up from the last crumbs of the last dessert. "This was the greatest meal I've ever eaten," he said.

"You ate *all* of them?" the waiter asked, pointing to the dessert cart.

"Not me," said Justin. "We shared them. They were terrific."

We got the bill, and I realized that although all our parents had remembered about extra money for a tip, none of them had thought about the tax that would be added. As a result, much of the money that was meant for the tip had to go to pay our bill.

When my father came to pick us up, I explained the situation to him. He reached into his pocket and pulled out a five-dollar bill.

"Should I ask him for change?" I wanted to know.

"No," he said.

On the way home Justin complained that he wasn't feeling well.

"Ghost fever," I suggested.

"Pig fever," said Alana.

"Can't be," moaned Justin. "I didn't eat any pork." But of course he'd eaten just about everything else.

2
Nature Takes Its Course

No matter what the calendar claims, winter in Vermont starts at the end of October and doesn't end until March or April. We get loads of snow, and every year I make a snowman for my sister. This year, because of Mom's pregnancy, my father worried all the time that she would slip and fall on the ice when she went outside. So he kept me shoveling a good path to our car. I had to wake up half an hour earlier each morning, just to be sure I had enough time for shoveling and feeding the llamas. I hated the shoveling, but the llamas always put me back in a good mood.

Even though they couldn't make snowballs or go skiing or do any of the other snow activities, the llamas loved the snow. They spent a lot of time outside their shed, and they exhaled thick clouds of steam. I attached our old sled to Ethan Allen's halter, and he pulled April along. "Don't be jealous," I told Ira. "Next year we'll have a new baby, and I'll pick up an old sled at the flea market or at a tag sale. Then you can take someone for rides too."

Justin celebrates Christmas, and my family celebrates Hanukkah. But we both got the same present this year—snowshoes! We had a great time tracking through the woods in them. I was surprised to discover that Alana's family celebrates both holidays. That's because one parent is Christian and one is Jewish. "Wow. Does that mean you get twice as many presents?" I asked her as she tried out my new snowshoes.

"No," she said, taking them off. "But I'm putting snowshoes on my list for next year. I want a pair."

Alana often came over to my house. She liked to do things with me, and she had loads of patience to play with April too. My mom was happy to let Alana cut out paper dolls or braid April's hair or whatever else kept my little sister busy. That's why Alana happened to spend the night of March 31 in a sleeping bag on the floor of April's bedroom. Alana's parents had driven up to visit her sister at college in Burlington that weekend, and they planned to stay overnight at a motel.

When Justin's mom called on Monday morning, April 1, to notify us that schools were closed, Alana and I cheered. There was no fresh snow outside, but there was plenty of mud. We could hardly believe the news. Despite 147 inches of snow (not all at once, of course), we hadn't missed a single day of school. The plows and the sanders always kept the roads open. Even the morning we woke to 19 inches, school had not been closed.

"First the milk trucks couldn't get out to get the milk from the farms," Justin's mother reported. "Then the bus drivers complained that they didn't think they could get the buses to complete their routes. Everyone says this is the worst mud season they can remember. And that's no April Fool's joke!"

"Thanks for calling. I'll pass the word on to the Hendersons," my mom said. The parents have a phone chain and one person calls another when there's an unexpected school closing.

"Mud season is here," I explained to Alana.

This was her first spring in Vermont. "What happens is that the thawing makes driving on dirt roads impossible. Cars get stuck in the mud, sort of like the quicksand scenes you see in the movies. I never heard of anyone getting killed in the mud, but it sure makes life inconvenient if your car's brakes need to be replaced because they became packed with mud."

It seemed like a holiday, eating breakfast in my pajamas the way I sometimes do on the weekend. I wasn't even self-conscious to have Alana see me that way. Besides, she was wearing her flannel pajamas too while happily putting dandelion jelly on a slice of toast. It feels as if she's part of our family.

"This is the greatest," she said, licking a bit of jelly off her fingers. I remembered how Justin had reacted to that very same homemade jam, and smiled. Alana was a much better guest, I thought.

Dad said that he was expecting an early-morning delivery from a carpet warehouse in New Hampshire. "Since they're driving on state highways, I'm pretty sure they'll make it," he told us.

"Drive carefully," Mom said. She stood up and put her arms around Dad. She was so big, with the baby inside her, that she couldn't get very close to him.

"Don't worry," Dad said over his shoulder as he left. "No one ever got hurt from mud."

"Adam," Mom said, turning to me, "put on some clothes. I'm going to put your pjs in the wash this morning."

"Okay," I answered as I drained the last of my milk.

Alana and April went off together to get dressed too. As I knotted the laces of my sneaks, I thought about calling Justin. Maybe he could join us on our unexpected holiday from school. Then I realized that if the buses didn't think they could make it through the mud, there was no way Justin's father would want to drive him over. As for biking, forget it.

Maybe Alana and I could bake cookies this morning, I thought. That would be fun.

"Adam? Adam, where are you?" I suddenly heard my mom calling me from the kitchen.

"Here I am," I responded, coming from my room. "Where did you think I—" I stopped in the middle of my sentence. My mother was standing bent over the kitchen table, and her face looked pale.

"Mom," I asked, "are you all right?"

She nodded her head, but she sure didn't look okay to me.

"Help April find a nice cartoon program on the TV," she said. That was the best proof of all that something was wrong. My mom is always discouraging us from sitting in front of the television set. And a *nice* cartoon program? She says too many cartoons will rot your brains.

"Are you sick?" I asked my mother anxiously.

"Not sick," she said, trying hard to smile.

"It's the baby, isn't it?" said Alana, who had joined us.

My mother nodded.

The baby? In a state of panic I ran to find April. I sat her down in front of the TV. She didn't know anything out of the ordinary was happening. She sat happily on the couch and put her thumb in her mouth. I left her watching *The Flintstones* and ran back to my mother. She was sitting at the kitchen table.

"Your mother is getting cramps," Alana whispered to me. "She says they're quite strong. That means the baby's on its way."

"When?" I asked dumbly.

"Now," my mom answered.

I knew the baby was due in the next ten days, but I wasn't expecting anything to happen when I was at home with my mom and my dad wasn't.

"What can we do to help?" Alana asked.

I looked at her gratefully. I wasn't alone. But even though we'd both seen that sex education film at school, what did we really know about childbirth?

Mom bit her lip and looked as if she were trying not to say anything.

"I can't reach your father," she said after a minute. "So I called the medical center, and they said they'd try to get someone over here as soon as possible.

"Call Dad again for me," she said, handing me the telephone receiver. "Maybe he's reached the store by now."

I pushed the buttons quickly. There was no answer. "He could still be on his way to the store," I said. "Or maybe he ran out for a cup of coffee. Or maybe . . ."

"Maybe he's stuck in the mud," Alana said, remembering what I'd told her about the dangers of mud season. I knew she must be right.

"I guess you'll just have to wait," I said helplessly.

"That's the first thing you learn about babies. They don't wait. They come when they're ready," Mom said.

She started to pull herself up from her chair, and Alana gave her an arm for support. "I'm going to need your help, kids," she said as she led the way into Dad's and her bedroom. Mom lay down on their bed.

"How are you feeling now?" I asked, but my voice came out in a squeaky nervous tone.

"All right at this moment," Mom said. "But put the radio on. I want some loud music."

"What's that for?" I wanted to know.

"It will muffle the noise if I shout out. I don't want to scare April."

Mom's words scared *me*. "What's going to happen?" I asked.

"Nothing, I hope," Mom replied. "But it's just possible that the baby is going to be born right here in our house instead of in the hospital as planned."

"Oh, Mrs. Fine!" Alana gasped, and I watched the color drain out of her face. "That's the most amazing thing I ever heard."

My mother smiled at Alana, but then her expression changed as another cramp went through her body.

We watched her carefully and saw her relax as the pain eased up. "How often are the contractions coming?" Alana asked.

That impressed me. I didn't even know the word *contraction*.

"I'm not sure," my mother said. She turned to

face the little digital clock on the bedside table. "Maybe you'd both better go wash your hands," she said.

Nobody had ever washed better than we did that morning. The longer we soaped up our fingers and rinsed them off, the more likely it would be that the people from the medical center would arrive at our house. What did we know about delivering a baby? Nothing. *N-o-t-h-i-n-g.* Suppose we messed up. What would happen to Mom? And what about my baby brother?

I don't remember either of us saying a single word to each other the entire time we were scrubbing our hands. I guess Alana felt just as frightened by the responsibility as I did. Finally we dried our hands and returned to the bedroom. Mom had changed back into her nightgown.

"Adam, fill the teakettle with water, and put it on to boil," she told me. "And the big spaghetti pot too," she added. I was relieved to run out of the room. If only there were many things I could do away from my mother, yet still help her during this terrible period. When the teakettle and pot were filled with water and on the stove, I stopped to check on April. She was completely absorbed by the crazy antics of Fred and Wilma Flintstone. She had no idea that anything else was happening in the world.

I couldn't stall anymore, so I returned to my parents' bedroom. There was loud music coming from the radio, but I could still hear my mother's voice calling out, "Oh. Oh. Oh."

I looked at Alana. Wasn't there anything we could do? "How about aspirin?" I said.

Alana turned and saw me. She came toward the door and said, "Go call the medical center again. And call your father too. Maybe you'll reach him now. Tell them that the contractions are only five minutes apart."

"Is that good? Or is that bad?" I asked helplessly.

"It's fine," Alana said. "It's just happening much faster than you'd expect. They say that for some women each baby comes faster than the one before."

I was in awe of how calm Alana sounded about all this. Maybe the girls had seen a different video from the one the boys had, I thought. Or maybe it was in the female genes. After all, female cats and dogs and horses know what to do. Maybe girls and mothers do too.

I started to go into the bedroom, toward the phone near the bed, but Alana pushed me away. "Do it in the kitchen," she shouted to me. "You'll hear better."

"Oh. Oh. Oh," my mother called out once again over the sound of the music.

"Oh. Oh. Oh." I heard it again. This time I didn't know if the sounds were coming from me or from my mother.

I felt like a coward, leaving Alana alone with my mother, but I was thrilled to have another assignment out of that bedroom.

Back in the kitchen the air was all steamy, and there was the shrill whistle of the teakettle. The water had already boiled. The spaghetti pot was beginning to boil too. I turned the two gas burners down very low. I glanced at the kitchen clock and was amazed to see that it was almost ten-thirty. Dad would certainly be at the store by now, I thought.

But then I decided I'd better call the medical center first. Luckily the number was right there on the wall next to the phone. I punched in all the numbers and waited impatiently as the phone rang six times before someone picked it up. Six rings? What were they doing there?

"Deerfield Valley Medical Center," a voice finally responded.

"When are you coming?" I asked. "The contractions are every five seconds. I mean minutes. But maybe by now they *are* seconds!"

I know I sounded all rattled and confused. But that's how I was.

"Who's calling, please?" the voice at the medical center asked.

"It's me. Adam. Adam Fine. My mother's having the baby. Right this minute. Why aren't you here?"

"Adam, please keep calm," the voice said to me. "An ambulance is on its way to your house at this very instant. It may be turning into your driveway even as we speak."

I pulled on the phone cord as far as it would go and looked out the kitchen window. "There's no ambulance in our driveway!" I shouted into the phone.

"Then it will be there any minute. Just relax. Everything will be fine."

"Fine? Fine?" I wasn't fine at all even if that's my name. I began giggling at the thought. Adam Fine isn't feeling fine.

I turned on the kitchen faucet and filled a glass with water. My mouth felt dry from all the tension, and I gulped it down quickly.

Then, forgetting to call my father, I ran back upstairs to see how my mother was doing. It was awful that I'd abandoned her and Alana. But over the noise of the music I could suddenly hear another sound. It was a baby crying. How could that be?

My mother and Alana were not alone. Half-wrapped in a towel but still attached to my mother by the umbilical cord was my baby brother. At least I thought it was a brother until Alana gave me the news.

"Adam," she said in voice filled with emotion, "you have a new sister. And I helped deliver her!"

The baby was covered with blood and seemed as wet and slippery as the muddy roads outside. But she was so beautiful, with tiny features and limbs, that I wasn't even disgusted by the sight. When we saw the film at school, we all said it was gross. But here in the room with Mom and the baby it was the coolest and most beautiful thing I'd ever seen in my life.

I leaned over and wiped the baby's face with a corner of the towel. I couldn't believe that this crying baby had arrived magically into our home and into our lives while I was talking on the telephone in our kitchen.

"Now you have to cut the umbilical cord," said Mom. She was half sitting up, leaning on a pair of pillows. Her eyes were shining, and there was a happy smile on her face.

"Cut?" I asked. I looked at Alana, and she

looked at me. I didn't think either of us could cut anything. The umbilical cord was about as thick as my middle finger. How in the world could I cut it? Could Alana do it?

"Take the shoelace out of your sneaker," Mom said to me. It sounded crazy, but there amid the noise of the crying baby and the loud music I kicked off one of my sneakers and took the lace out of it.

"Now tie the lace as tightly as you can near the baby's navel," she said.

I did that. "Doesn't it hurt?" I asked.

Mom shook her head and smiled. "No. Now go downstairs and get a knife from the kitchen," she said. She was cradling the baby in her arms. "Get a sharp one. The one I use for slicing—"

Thank goodness I didn't have to cut anything. At that moment April came running to the bedroom.

"There's people outside the house," she said, standing in the doorway. Then her eyes grew wide with disbelief. "When did the baby come?" she asked us.

"In the middle of *The Flintstones*," I shouted, running down the stairs to let the public health nurse in the door.

After she had attended to my mother, the

nurse turned to Alana. "Did you realize what you were doing?" she asked as she patted Alana on the back.

"Yep. But don't worry. I won't take your job away. I don't make house calls like you do," she said.

"Why didn't you call me?" asked Dad, who had suddenly arrived home.

"We did. Twice. You weren't there."

"I'm buying a car phone," said Dad. "Tomorrow."

The rest of the morning became a blur. Alana and I were exhausted from the experience, and Mom was too. So was the baby. Mom and the baby both slept, but Alana and I had to keep answering questions from everyone. Somehow another phone chain started, and neighbors called for hours to offer congratulations and to marvel at what had happened.

"Were you freaked out?" asked Justin. "Was it disgusting?"

"No," I said. I didn't try to explain things to him. He'd seen the film the same as I had. But seeing a film and seeing the real thing are as different as Vermont in mud season and Vermont in July.

Later in the day, after Alana's parents had returned to town and picked her up, things began to calm down. But poor April was still confused about the arrival of the baby, and I couldn't blame her a bit. *I* was confused, and I'd been there the whole time.

"What's our baby's name?" asked April.

"Well. We can't call her April, even though she was born in April," said Mom, leaning over to kiss April. "One April in a family is enough."

April's birthday is in July, so Dad said, "We could call her July. That would really confuse people!"

"We need another *A* name," said Mom. "It's three years since Grandma Gussie passed away, and it would be a tribute to her memory to use her name, or at least her first initial."

Grandma Gussie was my father's mother. Her real name was Augusta, and she was the one who cooked chicken livers.

"If we had an Augusta and an April in our family, it would sound like a calendar," Dad said, forgetting that two minutes before he had joked about naming the baby July.

"How about Arlene? Angela? Annette?" Mom continued.

"Didn't you think about names before this?" I asked with disbelief.

"We talked about names, but it's not the same as giving a name to a baby in your arms," Mom explained. "Before you were born, we called you Peter and Gregory and Matthew. Then, when I saw you for the first time, I said, 'Adam.' And you became Adam ever after."

Even though my mother claims she named me Adam on a whim, I also know that she was very fond of her Grandfather Avram, and the *A* initial of my name is in his memory.

"I know an *A* name that we should use," I said slowly.

"What is it?" demanded April.

I blushed a little before I said it. "How about the name Alana?" I suggested. "We wouldn't really be naming the baby for Alana, but we'd be borrowing her name and honoring the memory of Grandma Gussie at the same time."

"Of course! Why didn't I think of it myself?" said Mom, looking down at the baby. "In fact it's perfect." She looked at Dad to see if he agreed.

"I like it too," he said. "And it's a wonderful thank-you to Alana Brown for her help in delivering this young lady."

So that is how we came to have Alana in the family.

One more thing happened as a result of Alana's birth. A photographer from the *Valley News* arranged to take a picture of Alana Brown holding Alana Fine. It was on page three, and just in case there was anyone left in town who hadn't heard the story of the home birth assisted by a fifth-grade student, there it all was spelled out in great detail. The picture is great, and I have a copy of it hanging on the bulletin board in my bedroom. But I was a little disappointed that the photographer didn't want me to be in the picture too. After all, I'd been part of all that action even if I hadn't been in the room at the exact minute that the baby was born.

There's one more thing that bothers me. I never found out what were we going to use all that boiling water for anyhow.

10
A Llama in the Library

So suddenly I was among the older people in my family, with two little sisters to watch out for. It made me feel much older, even before my birthday added another year to my age. And now it was spring again too. Baby Alana was almost a month old, and we'd all started calling her Lani so as not to confuse her with the other Alana. One evening the phone rang. My father answered it, and then he called to me.

"Your books must be terribly overdue," he said. "It's Ms. Walsh from the public library asking to speak to you."

I hadn't been to the library in weeks, and I didn't have any books out at all, so for a fraction of a moment I couldn't imagine what he was talking about. But then it came to me.

"You didn't forget that you offered to have your llamas come for the grand reopening of the library, did you?" she asked me.

"Of course not," I said.

"We've set the date for the ceremony for Sunday, May nineteenth. Even though we're not usually open on Sunday, it's a day when the largest number of people will be able to attend. Besides, I'm hoping that sometime in the not-so-distant future I will be able to offer library service seven days a week."

"We'll be there," I said. I was really looking forward to showing off Ethan and Ira Allen to everyone.

"Great," said Ms. Walsh. "I'm going to print a flyer and get a press release out. It will make a big difference if I can count on the llamas being there."

"Almost as good as the president coming," I said.

"Adam, you're brilliant. Why didn't I think of it?" she shrieked into the phone.

"What did I say?" I asked. Then, remembering, I said, "Oh, forget it, Ms. Walsh. There's no way the president of the United States will come to the library reopening."

"I know that," Ms. Walsh said. "But I'll invite the president of every local organization. I can advertise that ten or fifteen presidents will be present. But you also gave me another idea. This is an election year. I might be able to get the governor to come."

"You really think so?" I asked. I was very impressed.

"It doesn't hurt to try. And I wouldn't even have thought of it if you hadn't given me the idea."

It was nice of Ms. Walsh to give me credit. But I couldn't really see the connection between my few words and her big plan.

Just as she promised, Ms. Walsh began publicizing the reopening. There was an article about the ceremony in the weekly paper and also one in the *Brattleboro Reformer,* which is published every day. There were signs up everywhere: in the supermarket, gas station, post office, Laundromat, bank, bakery. If you knew how to read, you knew about the celebration.

"What costume are you going to wear?" Justin asked me. Even though his interest in ghosts seemed to have faded since he'd been trapped in the secret stairway at the White House, he decided that he'd put a sheet over his head. "It's the easiest costume in the world," he said.

"Boring," I told him. "I thought we were going as book characters."

"We're too old for that Humpty Dumpty stuff," he said, referring to a pair of costumes our mothers made for us one Halloween when we were little.

"Why don't you go as Johnny Appleseed?" I suggested. "There are a couple of books about him in the library. You could wear one of your mother's pots on your head and carry a sack of apples. That's pretty easy, and it will look more interesting."

Justin liked the idea of the pot. "I'd be able to see better without a sheet over my face, and I can eat better too," he admitted. "What about you?"

"I'm thinking of going as a gaucho," I told him.

"Huh?" Justin responded.

"That's a South American cowboy," I explained. "One of my mother's friends gave her an old straw sombrero as a joke. And with a bandanna around my neck and holding on to a rope attached to the halter of one of our llamas, I'll look perfect."

"What book is that in?"

He had me there. "You can hold the other llama even if you're not a gaucho," I offered, ignoring his question. "My mom will have Lani, and Alana said she'd an keep eye on April. My dad will probably want to go around talking to all his friends. They're really expecting a mob at the library."

Alana said she had a red cape that she could wear and be Little Red Riding Hood. If any other fifth-grade girl had said that, I would have thought it was babyish. But I knew she'd look more beautiful than ever.

"Great!" I told her.

All the local restaurants and inns were donating cakes and cookies. There would be fruit punch for the kids and coffee for the adults. It was going to be terrific as long as it didn't rain. Even with the expanded quarters, there was no way the library could hold everyone plus the llamas. And maybe even the governor. Ms. Walsh told me that she had received a call from his office saying he would make every effort to attend the event.

Luckily, on Sunday, May 19, the sun was shining. After breakfast I brushed both llamas so they'd look their best. Then I went into the house and took a shower. I wanted to be extra clean in case I got a chance to shake hands with the governor. April, on the other hand, had green paint

on her fingers. She had spent the morning helping my father paint the fence along the edge of
our property. Now she was wearing her Raggedy
Ann costume, left over from Halloween.

"Ethan Allen looks funny," she announced to
me.

"Don't be silly," I said. "I just brushed him. He
looks wonderful."

"He's turning green!" April insisted.

Something inside me said I'd better go check.
I stuffed the remains of the sandwich I was eating
into my mouth and ran outside.

I could hardly believe my eyes. April was right.
Since the time I'd groomed him, Ethan Allen had
gone to inspect the freshly painted fence closely.
Now there were bright green stripes going down
one side of his body.

Any other day I would have laughed at my
llama's attempt to disguise himself as a zebra. But
not on the day of the reopening of the public
library. I wanted Ethan Allen's white wool hair to
gleam. He looked ridiculous with green stripes.

I could think of two alternatives—paint
remover or a scissors. A scissors would be faster
and smell better too. But how would my llama
look with a haircut on just one side of his body?

I ran to ask my parents for advice.

"You don't have enough time to give Ethan

Allen a haircut or to try to remove the paint," Mom commented, looking at the clock. She went over to a chest of drawers and pulled out a red-and-white-checked tablecloth. "Fold this in half and put it over his back," she instructed me. "It will hide the paint."

My dad drove us into town in our pickup truck. My mother and the baby sat in front with him and April, and I rode in the back with the llamas. I'd tied the ribbons from Alana around their halters, and what with the red-and-white table-cloth over Ethan Allen, they were looking really fantastic. Maybe we'd have to start putting table-cloths over both llamas whenever my mom went on one of her treks. The cloths could also be used when the tourists ate their picnic lunch.

We met Justin and Alana outside the library. Alana was cute with the red cape on. She was holding a little basket too. And Justin looked pretty comical with his mother's cooking pot on his head. My sombrero looked a whole lot better than his pot.

Ms. Walsh was standing in front of the library, waiting for me. She was dressed in an old-fashioned outfit, and her skirts reached the ground. She jumped up and down and clapped her hands with excitement when she saw us.

My father parked the pickup and arranged the plank that we use as a ramp for the llamas. The actual program wasn't scheduled to begin until one o'clock, but there were already people gathering outside the library, watching us. I led Ira Allen down the ramp and then Ethan Allen. I handed Ira Allen over to Justin. He was going to stand outside the front entrance with the llama. Even though Ms. Walsh was still a bit nervous about the idea, the plan was that Ethan Allen would actually go *inside* the library.

My father was about to place the plank against the front steps of the building, but Ms. Walsh stopped him. "We've added a handicap access during the renovation," she pointed out. "It's also an excellent llama access."

The library celebration was like Fourth of July, the flea market, and the Farmer's Day Fair all rolled into one. Everyone I ever knew in town was there. After all, when else would they get a free piece of cake made by some of those expensive tourist inns and restaurants?

I was so proud of Ethan Allen. Many people posed to have their photos taken standing next to him, and he didn't soil the new library carpeting (which my father had donated at cost). Everyone was curious to see a llama up close. And it wasn't only the kids. One man came over and started asking me a load of questions.

By now I'm a real expert, so I could tell him everything he wanted to know, like how llamas are mostly found in the Andes of South America but that now there are many llama farms throughout the United States. "There are hundreds of llamas in Vermont these days," I informed him.

The man thanked me and shook my hand, and someone flashed our picture. There were so many pictures taken that I didn't even remember that moment until the next day. It was printed on the front page of the *Brattleboro Reformer*. It shows me, in the sombrero, holding the rope attached to Ethan Allen's halter. My right hand is shaking the man's hand. I didn't know it at the time, but that man was the governor of the state of Vermont.

I saw the picture at school. The principal came in with the newspaper and held it up for everyone in my class to see. In the evening my dad came home from work holding a stack of newspapers. He wants to mail them to all our relatives. I must confess, it's pretty exciting to see your face on the *front page* of the newspaper. I guess the governor wasn't so impressed. It's happened to him before. But for me and Ethan Allen, it was a first.

Even though her picture had been in the

A Llama in the Library

Mixed Review
Afternoon in P

Flower Hill Boa
Metricom Prese

paper less than two months before, Alana also was very excited. "The *Brattleboro Reformer* is a daily paper," she exclaimed. "It's much more important than a weekly."

Justin was a little disappointed that he and Ira Allen didn't get their picture in the paper too. But he was distracted by an interesting piece of information he had picked up the day of the library reopening. He'd heard someone talking about how there'd once been a town where Lake Whitingham is now. The lake was really a man-made reservoir, and to build it, they'd flooded over the entire community. As far as Justin was concerned, if ever there was a place to go hunting for ghosts, it was down by the lake. So I know what he's planning for us to do during the coming summer.

But before then there are other things happening. The fifth grade is going to take a trip to Boston. We're going to see the Old North Church, where a light was placed during the American Revolution to let Paul Revere know whether the British were coming by land or by sea. And one day soon Alana is going to come over and help me gather all the dandelions on our property. She offered to do it if I'd help her pick them around her home. Then she wants to help my mother cook dandelion jelly, so she can learn how to make it too.

"It's so delicious, and it looks like bottled gold," she said.

You can be sure I'll never tell her what Justin called it.